RACE TO THE MOONRISE

AN ANCIENT JOURNEY

Written by Sally Crum
Illustrated by Eric S. Carlson

D1113552

WESTERN REFLECTIONS PUBLISHING COMPANY®
Montrose, CO

Second Edition
Printed in the U.S.A.

ISBN 13: 978-1-932738-31-5
ISBN 10: 1-932738-31-2

Library of Congress Control Number: 2005938638

Cover and interior illustrations by Eric S. Carlson

Cover and book design: Laurie Goralka Design

Western Reflections Publishing Company®
219 Main Street
Montrose, CO 81401
www.westernreflectionspub.com

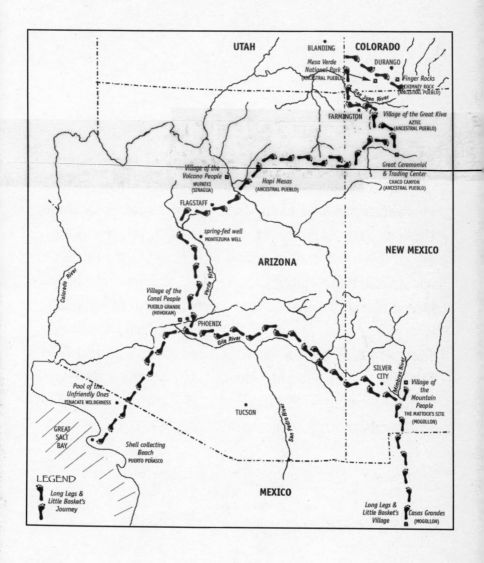

Acknowledgments

Several archaeologists reviewed the story and I am grateful for their suggestions and comments. They include Linda Martin, Kathy Fiero, and Joe Brisbin of Mesa Verde National Park; Cory Breternitz of Soil Systems, Inc.; Kathy Reigle and other staff members of Pueblo Grande Museum; and friends Gary Matlock, Sally Cole, and Terri Liestman. Fine editorial assistance was offered by Danni Langdon, Jan Ryan, JaneFitz-Randolph, and Barbara Springer. Thanks to Bill Hoy, Harriet Walck, and Mom, Dad, and Pete for their moral support. Thanks also to the Intertribal Cultural Committee of the Council for Indian Education for their support and endorsement.

Preface

In 1200 A.D., most people living in what we know today as northern Mexico and the southwestern United States were farmers in small villages or large towns. Although they spoke different languages, they shared many traits. Farming methods and ceremonies that brought rain to the crops, along with useful tools and ornamental jewelry, were passed from one group to another, from Mexico to southern Colorado.

Traders were athletes, trained from childhood to run long distances while carrying heavy loads, traveling perhaps 15 to 40 miles each day. Seasoned traders may have spoken many languages fluently; others probably used sign language to communicate with their customers.

The peoples visited by the traders in this story belong to the cultures archaeologists call the Mogollon (Mo-go-YON), or Mountain People, of southwestern New Mexico; the Hohokam (HO-ho-KAM), or Canal People, of the Phoenix Basin; the Sinagua (Seen-AH-Gua), or Volcano People, who lived close to the San Francisco Peaks (near Flagstaff); the Hopi (HOPE-ee), people who still live today on the Hopi Mesas east of Flagstaff; and the Ancestral Puebloans (formerly called the Anasazi) of the Four Corners area—where Arizona, Utah, Colorado, and New Mexico share a common corner.

Archaeologists can date artifacts fairly well, and those described in the story are represented as accurately as possible. Religious ceremonies and ideas are more difficult to date, so some of the events in the story, such as the ball court game and the Ladder Dance, may have occurred slightly before and after the time of this tale.

Chapter 1

Northern Mexico,
Early Spring,
A.D. 1200

Long Legs thought his lungs would burst as he veered around the cactus and ran toward the desert village. In all his twelve years, he had never passed his uncle on the trail, but this evening he was gaining on him. Suddenly, Uncle stumbled and fell flat, and Long Legs, close behind, tripped over him. The boy's backpack full of rocks thudded painfully against his bare back, as he broke his fall with his arms.

"Uncle! What happened?" cried Long Legs, panting hard and pulling the hair from his eyes.

"My legs gave out again, but I'm fine. I'm still the fastest runner in the village. But you, my strong nephew, are almost as swift!"

Uncle brushed sand from his lanky body, then limped to a nearby dry wash. He picked up two large cobbles and brought them back.

"You can carry more weight now that you run so fast." He put the stones in Long Legs' deer-hide pack. "After this practice you can travel with me on any trading venture and carry all my trade goods!" His weathered, leathery face wrinkled around his merry eyes. He became serious and added, "Your father would be proud."

Long Legs thought sadly of his father, also a trader. A year ago he had left to trade in the Far North, and they had not seen him since.

Beyond the cluster of mud houses, the sun was setting in blaze orange as the two runners trotted toward their hometown. "I hear drums," said Long Legs. Listening to the rhythmic pounding he added, "They tell of visitors from far away."

Entering the village, they flung their sweating bodies by the canal that brought spring water to the houses. "Don't drink so fast; you'll get a cramp," said Uncle as Long Legs dipped handful after handful of water from the canal and slurped. The boy then dunked his entire head into the canal and tossed back his wet hair. It slapped his back, reaching almost to his waist.

Across the plaza a girl ran toward them. It was Little Basket, Long Legs' ten-year-old sister. He smiled as he watched her lope easily across the plaza, her long braids flying behind her. She runs as I do, he thought.

"Long Legs, Uncle, come quickly!" she said, her brown eyes flashing with excitement. "There are travelers from the Far North in our house. Perhaps they have word of our father!"

Long Legs' thoughts were jumbled. Last night in their family sleeping room Little Basket had awakened him. "I dreamed that strange people from far away came to our town," she had said. She often had dreams foretelling the future, and, though it made her feel uncomfortable, she was considered to have special medicine powers.

Long Legs bounded after his sister. He recalled with pride how she was the youngest child in the history of the village to be trained as a medicine woman. Distant towns requested her to attend their ceremonies. Through her dreams she predicted if rain would come to water the crops or if an injured person would survive. Long Legs thought of the small offerings Little Basket made when she visited other villages. Her gifts of pretty rocks or tiny doll baskets always brought the villagers good luck. She is one of the most favored people in the land, he thought.

That morning, when their mother heard of Little Basket's dream of visitors, she began to grind extra corn. She had spent much of the day making corn patties and had asked Long Legs to kill a fat rabbit to make a large pot of stew.

As they entered the low doorway of their tiny mud-walled house, Long Legs saw three men squatting on the yucca mats. They reminded him of how his father looked after a long trading trip—dark brown from weeks in the sun and lean from eating mostly trail food of corn, gruel, nuts, and an occasional rabbit. The soles of their feet were callused from running great distances barefoot.

"Thank the gods you're here, my brother," Long Legs' mother said to Uncle. "They don't speak our language very well, and Little Basket and I don't speak theirs at all!"

She nervously picked up some brown bowls from her kitchen area and handed them to Little Basket who ladled out the stew from a large gray cooking pot. Mother shyly handed the bowls to the guests. The men gratefully gulped down the stew, wiping the bowls clean with great chunks of corn patties. They politely belched their appreciation.

When all were finished eating, Uncle cleared his throat. "Honored guests," he began. "You are tired from your long journey. Sleep and we shall talk tomorrow." He started to rise, but Mother looked at him pleadingly.

She hopes to hear news of Father, Long Legs thought.

A visitor, wearing long turquoise earrings, spoke. "We have no time to wait. We bring a request from our most powerful priest, Thunder Voice." Mother looked at Long Legs. Uncle had taught him many languages of the people with whom he traded. Long Legs shook his head, letting her know they were not speaking of Father. She rose and gathered up the empty food bowls.

The youngest guest, not much older than Long Legs, continued. "As you probably have heard, the gods are displeased with our people of the Far North. The farm fields near our great Ceremonial and Trading Center no longer produce fine corn, beans, and squash and now are abandoned. Our underground kivas that once throbbed with the beat of pounding drums are silent."

The third traveler, an old man who looked to Long Legs to be almost thirty-five, twisted his long gray hair.

Long Legs thought Uncle must be nearing his age. "The rest of us in other villages of the Far North are starting to fight among ourselves for food. The deer are disappearing, and we have little wood for fuel and building materials."

Long Legs could no longer keep quiet. In halting phrases that his uncle had taught him he spoke the strange language. "What does this have to do with us? Have you heard of our father?" Uncle glared at him.

The old man looked sharply at Long Legs, but he spoke gently. "I know nothing of your father. But someone from your village must have been in our area, because we have heard of the powers of your sister, Little Basket."

Long Legs glanced at Little Basket. Her face showed no emotion, but he felt her hand grab his as she heard her name amid the strange words.

The old trader looked straight at Long Legs. "Less than five moons from now our most powerful priests will travel to a place called Finger Rocks, a deserted village high on a mesa top. The gods make the moon rise between the tall Finger Rocks every nineteen autumns. The priests say that with the proper offerings on the twentieth night of the Month of the Falling Leaves, the sacred Moonrise will occur." His narrow eyes darted to Little Basket.

"Why is he looking at me?" she whispered to Long Legs. Mother looked anxiously at the strangers.

"If the gods are pleased with us, they show it by stopping the moon as it rises. The moon stands still between the narrow peaks."

Long Legs translated to Little Basket. Her eyes grew wide.

"Thunder Voice and our other most powerful priests request the presence of the medicine girl at the Moonrise. Her offerings will impress the gods. The gods may tell her the future of our people. We bring a pack full of turquoise jewelry to pay for her services." The man lifted the flap of his pack and dug out a handful of beautiful necklaces.

Uncle translated the stranger's request to Mother.

"I won't allow her to travel that far! I have already lost a husband," she said. Her face showed her fear.

Long Legs hastily spoke up. "But, Mother, Uncle and I could escort her to Finger Rocks and find out what happened to Father! Besides, Uncle has trained me well, and I need the experience of trading with other people."

Mother stared sadly at Little Basket. After a long while she turned to Uncle. "The village elders must make a final decision. If they say she must go, then she must go, but please bring my children back to me," she said quietly, "and also my husband."

Chapter 2

That night, Uncle went to his clan's kiva to discuss whether the children should make the long trip to help the Far North People. Long Legs lay awake on his rabbit fur blanket until Uncle crept into the house. Before he had made it all the way through the door, Long Legs whispered anxiously, "What did the elders decide?"

Uncle drew the rest of his body through the small T-shaped doorway and said, "All of them have heard of the priest, Thunder Voice. His powers are known far and wide. The elders fear that if Little Basket does not attend the Moonrise, Thunder Voice will invoke the gods to punish our village. They say she must go."

Long Legs slept restlessly the remainder of the night. When the mud-walled room became light enough to see, he woke Little Basket. They grabbed their backpacks, which they had filled the night before, and raced to the town plaza.

It was already a scene of frenzied activity. The visitors from the Far North were going back home, and villagers wanted to hear all the news before they departed.

It would probably be a long time before any people who lived that far away would visit again.

Also in the plaza that morning were neighbors of Long Legs who had traveled to the Far North many times on trading ventures. Each gave Long Legs advice as to bartering with foreigners. The boy sensed they were jealous of his leaving on this great adventure without them.

Long Legs nervously rearranged his pack for the fourth time and thought about how nice it would be to carry real trade goods instead of rocks. He placed four balls of salt at the bottom of the pack. "Everyone likes salt in their rabbit stew," he mumbled. He put two small rubber balls on top of the salt. I've heard the people of the Far North don't play the ball court games, but maybe we'll visit others who do on the way there, he thought.

Last night his mother had given him several small copper bells. Many years before her father was born, her great-grandfather had brought them from the Great City to the south. They were valuable. Long Legs carefully wrapped the bells in cotton cloth and tucked them between the rubber balls. Shell bracelets, pouches of corn and mesquite flour, and dried deer meat filled the rest of his pack.

Little Basket bounced toward him, carrying a stick birdcage with a red and green macaw in it. "I picked up Squawk at the aviary. You are taking him, aren't you?" she asked. The huge bird of the parrot family was calmly preening his long, scarlet tail feathers, which almost touched the ground.

"Yes, he's more than a pet to me, so I don't want to trade him. But we could trade lots of his feathers," said Long Legs. "I've taught him so many words, I consider him a friend."

Squawk seemed disgusted. "Squawk good bird," he screeched.

Long Legs and Little Basket laughed. "We'll leave you enough feathers to keep you warm at night in the Far North," Long Legs told him.

"And I'll carry all the sunflower seeds you'll need to eat," added Little Basket.

Uncle and the three travelers from the Far North walked across the plaza to the children. Uncle looked upset. "We have a longer journey ahead than we thought," he said. "Our visitors have told me that Little Basket must take special offerings to present at the Moonrise."

The youngest traveler looked at Long Legs. "Thunder Voice requires a beautiful bowl from the Mountain People, an ancient clay doll from the Canal People, white clam shells from the Salt Bay, a fine cotton cape from the Volcano People, and a painted mug from the Cliff Dwellers of the Far North People. He thinks the gods will surely talk to Little Basket if the trouble is taken to obtain these offerings."

"But it will take several months to travel that far and to visit so many places!" blurted Long Legs.

"Thunder Voice demands it," replied the man with the earrings. "These offerings must be collected by Little Basket. You can help barter for them. It you don't obey, Thunder Voice will ask the gods to harm your village."

Long Legs remembered what the elders had said about Thunder Voice. They were right, he thought.

Uncle turned to Long Legs and Little Basket. "We must leave soon and keep a steady pace. We will visit the Mountain People first, but we can trade with them for only a day. We must then head west to the desert farms of the Canal People."

As Long Legs hurriedly tied the thongs to close his pack, the youngest visitor from the Far North approached him. "I'm sorry I didn't talk to you more last evening. My name is Raven Claw."

Long Legs looked curiously at the young man. Raven Claw continued, "I wish things were different, but my people are desperate. They need the powers of your sister. I wish you luck on your journey."

Long Legs nodded and said softly, "It's not your fault, Raven Claw. May the gods watch over you."

Mother hugged Uncle and her children, and, with a brave smile said, "Every night I will look at the Traveler's Star and know it is shining over my dear ones, leading them in the right direction."

Little Basket's eyes filled with tears. Long Legs helped her with her pack and said cheerily, "We'll be fine, Mother. And we may return with Father!"

The three visitors from the Far North ran ahead. They would travel straight north to home. As they moved farther away, the young one shouted back, "See you at the Moonrise Ceremony, Long Legs!" They were soon out of sight behind a low hill.

Uncle, Long Legs, and Little Basket broke into a jog and ran easily toward the river. Hundreds of trade shells sewn onto their cotton skirts clacked noisily. Their packs were full, because they wanted to take as many trade items as possible. With every step, Long Legs felt the thump of heavy shell necklaces against his bare chest and the pull of several pairs of turquoise earrings dangling from his ears. They felt uncomfortable. He hoped to trade them first.

The trail followed the river at the edge of the willows and cottonwood trees. It was just wide enough for the travelers to run single file.

Thousands of years of foot travel had worn it deep into the desert soil. Uncle said the trail had been used by the ancient hunters before they learned to farm and even before the great trade routes were established. Long Legs could not imagine a world without farming or trading.

Over his shoulder, Long Legs took a last, quick look back toward his village. He caught the eye of Little Basket, who was running behind him, and flashed her a reassuring grin. He then turned his thoughts toward breathing easily. They would jog steadily much of the day. "Even if we keep up this pace," he muttered, "will we arrive in time for the Moonrise Ceremony at Finger Rocks?"

Chapter 3

The third day on the trail, Uncle stumbled and fell, breaking one of the finely painted pots in his pack. "Tripped on a rock," he grumbled as Long Legs helped him up. But Long Legs could see no rocks on the trail big enough for him to trip over.

By evening, a large flat-topped mesa could be distinguished in the distance. A tall, pointed peak rose just east of it. "That's the land of the Mountain People," Uncle panted. "We'll be trading with them tomorrow."

Long Legs hoped he could trade his uncomfortable earrings for the pottery bowl Little Basket must offer at the Moonrise.

The next morning the spring sun rose hot over the jogging travelers. Long Legs looked wistfully at rain clouds moving around the peak ahead. He had not slept well, and the pack strap across his forehead was rubbing his skin raw. His feet, although tough, were sore after three days on the trail.

The trail had left the river the day before and now followed a dry streambed. By mid-morning, pools of water began to appear in the streambed, which was emerging from a wide canyon in front of them. As the group entered the canyon, Long Legs had an uneasy feeling that someone was watching them.

On a terrace of the canyon, Long Legs saw something move. "There's a house over there!" cried Little Basket. Figures emerged from the isolated mud-covered house and started down the slope toward them.

"What shall we do, Uncle?" asked Long Legs.

"Slow down a bit but keep running," Uncle replied. He drew a wooden flute from his waist pouch and began playing a lively tune. People were spilling from houses on both sides of the canyon. They hailed the travelers and filed in behind them.

The canyon widened into a broad valley. Long Legs noticed that the familiar desert shrubs of his homeland did not grow here. Instead, stunted pinyon pines and twisted juniper trees dotted the valley. Pine trees guarded the ridges above.

"There's a town ahead, by the stream," said Uncle. "We'll stop to trade there."

Still playing his flute, Uncle led the travelers into the plaza. People cheered and crowded around them. Long Legs noticed many of them staring at Little Basket, so he moved closer to her. "Don't be afraid. They're curious about a girl being with us—especially one carrying a macaw!" She tried to smile at the crowd.

Uncle whispered to the brother and sister, "Don't tell anyone why Little Basket is with us, other than to trade. You never know what someone might do to gain use of her powers."

As the travelers unloaded their packs in the plaza, the Mountain People brought out their trade items: skin pouches full of pinyon nuts; beautiful soft white buckskin; thick buffalo hides traded from the Plains People; and a few pottery bowls that looked old. On the inside of each bowl was painted a different animal design.

"Many people from our village moved here and married the local people. The religion of the Mountain People became more like ours," said Uncle. "They no longer make the painted bowls they put in the graves of their dead. Those bowls are now quite valuable."

Little Basket dragged Long Legs over to a woman displaying her bowls. "Look at this one with the long-eared rabbit!" Little Basket said. "Ask her if the rabbit design means anything."

Long Legs finally remembered the word for "rabbit" in the language of the Mountain People. Luckily, the word was not too different from their own. "What does the rabbit design mean?" he stammered.

The old woman laughed, her round, wrinkled face beaming. "The rabbit lives on the moon. You look right at him every time the moon is full."

When Long Legs translated, Little Basket said, "That will be perfect for the Moonrise! What will she trade for it?"

The woman eyed Squawk. "No, not the bird," said Long Legs, but we'll give you one of his feathers, a salt ball, and all the earrings I am wearing."

"Two feathers and the earrings," she said. "My grandson just returned from the Salt Bay. We have plenty of salt."

As Little Basket helped Long Legs put the bowl into his pack, it began to rain. The woman gathered up her pots. Just then, Uncle called to them from across the plaza. "Come, children! The village elder has invited us to stay the night with him." Long Legs and Little Basket thanked the woman and splashed across the plaza.

That night, their host told stories of Coyote, the trick-ster. At the end of each tale, he would look expectantly at Little Basket. Unable to understand most of the words he said, she would glance quickly at Long Legs who would wink at her, then burst into laughter. Little Basket would giggle politely; the old man would then slap his withered knee and again launch into another story. Little Basket soon fell asleep.

The fire cast shadows of the weary travelers on the walls of the room. Long Legs noticed that the walls were made of stacked river cobbles, not solid mud such as the walls in his house. The Mountain People are fortunate to have a river nearby with such good building rocks, he thought. He looked forward to all the new things he would learn on the trip.

Long Legs listened to the sounds of distant thunder, the crackling of the fire, and the storyteller's droning voice. Soon he felt his tired body slump. His eyes drooped and finally closed.

In the gray dawn the village elder said goodbye to the travelers. Uncle said to him, "We'd like to stay longer and swap trade goods and stories with your people. But we must leave this beautiful valley and get to the River of the Giant Lizard. It will lead us west to the towns of the Canal People."

From a ragged pouch the old man drew out two tiny turquoise figures—one of a bear and one of a rabbit. He gave the rabbit to Little Basket and the bear to Long Legs. Little Basket hugged the man and said, "Someday, I will understand your stories."

"Eh?" he said, as Long Legs gently pulled Little Basket away. As the group jogged out of town, Long Legs heard the old man say, "Did you hear about the time Coyote was fooled by Rattlesnake?" But his voice faded as they climbed the trail out of the valley.

After crossing many rolling hills of pinyon and juniper, they arrived at the River of the Giant Lizard. It was almost noon. The river emerged from the hills and slithered into a wide flood plain. In the distance, Long Legs saw bare mountains jutting toward the sky.

"Look at all the flowers!" cried Little Basket. Patches of orange poppies dotted the valley and golden blooms on green-barked trees blazed in the spring sunlight. On either side of the trail, white flowers decorated the tall stalks of yucca and century plants, all surrounded by shimmering, needle-pointed leaves.

For six days the travelers followed the river through the desert. On the seventh morning, Long Legs was awakened by the sorrowful coo of a mourning dove. An orange light shone over the jagged mountain to the east. Uncle had let them sleep late.

Next to him lay a sweaty lump, Little Basket. She had cried in her sleep again, and Long Legs wondered what horrors she was seeing. Maybe she's just homesick, he thought, as he gently pulled one of her long braids to wake her.

Little Basket's brown eyes searched his face until she recognized him. Long Legs felt sorry for her. Whenever the gods visited her in her dreams, she was not herself for hours. He pulled his long bangs aside so she could see him better. "I dreamed someone will be hurt today," she said softly, brushing the sand from her thin brown legs and arms.

"Sister, not all your dreams come true," Long Legs grumbled, but he wondered who it would be.

He yelped as he stood up, feeling the sharp clump of cholla cactus through his cotton skirt. Little Basket giggled and grabbed two river cobbles. "Hold still, the light is dim."

Long Legs winced as she yanked out the barbed spines of the jumping cactus, holding the cactus clump between the stones. "Maybe I was the one to get hurt," he moaned. Little Basket said nothing.

Chapter 4

For breakfast the travelers ate strips of dried rabbit and a thin gruel of water and mesquite bean flour. Uncle said to Long Legs, "Perhaps you and Little Basket can trade for an ancient clay doll with the Canal People today—if we hurry." After breakfast he helped Long Legs and Little Basket lift their heavy buckskin packs onto their backs and adjusted the carrying straps over their foreheads. Long Legs felt as if permanent creases had been worn there, even though Uncle had padded the straps with cattail down.

The sun peeked over the bleak mountain range and flooded the desert valley with light. Long fingers of ocotillo cast wavy shadows over rock-strewn sand.

Little Basket tossed some sunflower seeds and pinyon nuts into Squawk's cage of willow branches. She noticed Uncle's startled look. "Long Legs traded one of Squawk's feathers for the pinyon nuts before we left the Mountain People," she laughed, handing her uncle some of the nutritious seeds. He smiled and cracked one with his teeth, pulled out the white meat and popped it into his mouth.

"That bird will be naked by the time we reach the Finger Rocks if your brother keeps trading his feathers," he said.

"Squawk good bird," said Squawk.

Long Legs chuckled, picked up the cage, and walked briskly toward the river. He carefully avoided the sharp spines of the jumping cactus.

A large blue bird was standing on stick-like legs near the riverbank. Paying no attention to the group of humans, it accurately snatched a fish with its long bill.

Uncle took the lead, Little Basket followed, and Long Legs fell behind her. All morning they traveled without stopping. At midday they rested by a river pool and dangled their dusty legs in the cool water.

Long Legs noticed Little Basket looking intently at what appeared to be a colorful branch under a creosote bush at the edge of the river. She leaned to grab it.

"Aieeee!!" she shrieked. A black and coral splotched lizard the size of Long Legs' forearm clamped its jaws on her hand. Little Basket's dream flashed through Long Legs' mind.

"It's poisonous!" Uncle yelled, prying at the mighty jaws. But the Gila monster bit down harder and began to gnaw on Little Basket's hand. Uncle quickly picked up the girl and waded into the river, holding her arm under water. The lizard struggled fiercely, refusing to give up its death-like grip. Little Basket screamed in pain and terror.

Finally the lizard, unable to breathe, loosened its grip. Long Legs seized it by the tail and flung it to the other side of the river. Little Basket lay limp in Uncle's arms; when Uncle spoke to her, she did not answer.

Long Legs and Uncle took turns carrying Little Basket. The river trail passed small towns of mud huts. "The best medicine man will live at the Big Village," Uncle panted, trying to hold Little Basket steady as he ran. "We must get there soon."

Chapter 5

They entered a wide basin. From a low rise, Long Legs saw large villages clustered along the river. A system of wide canals and ditches formed a web of waterways that wove out from the villages. At regular points along the major canals, huge mounds of earth towered over the ditches.

"The canal overseers are the ones who supervise ditch construction and cleaning from atop these mounds," said Uncle as he ran. He glanced worriedly down at Little Basket and said no more.

Even now, he's trying to educate me about the Canal People, thought Long Legs. He looked lovingly as the old man jogged in front of him with Little Basket in his arms. Uncle will be as sad as I if she should die, he thought.

They followed the trail into the hazy basin, smoke from burning weeds and kitchen fires dimming the stark desert light. The river trail led them to a sprawling village situated beneath an outcrop of red rock. A tall mound like those along the canal systems loomed above all the houses in town.

"The medicine man should live on top of that mound," said Uncle. "'Take Little Basket. I must play the flute as we enter the village."

Uncle's flute songs sounded almost mournful. People cheered the colorful, approaching travelers until they saw Little Basket and the blood-soaked cloth that bound her hand. They immediately led the small party to the wall surrounding the mound. A surly, tattooed guard wearing a plumed headdress and carrying a huge club blocked the entrance to the mound area.

"The boy may not enter," he growled. Long Legs, unpracticed in the Language of the Canal People, thought he was not understanding the guard's words. He glanced questioningly at Uncle.

"Let the boy through. He is her brother!" Uncle said in the strange language. The guard sneered at Long Legs but let him pass.

"Follow me," he snarled as he led them to the top of the mound. He gestured to a small room of stone. "The medicine man lives here."

Stooping through the doorway, they entered the room. A withered old man muttered to himself as he cooked a foul-smelling brew over a fire. A shabby coyote skin covered his bony shoulders.

As Long Legs lowered Little Basket on a woven yucca mat, he struggled with the language. "We are traders from the South Country. My sister has been bitten by the Giant Lizard. Uncle and I will pay you well if you can cure her."

The old man's beady eyes glittered. "I will cure her. But you both must leave. Our village has challenged a neighboring town to a ball game. Go to the ball court and watch while I work my medicine!" he ordered, gathering various leaves, roots, and feathers from several worn leather pouches.

Long Legs did not want to leave Little Basket. Uncle nudged him and whispered, "Don't worry. He'll try to make her well; he has his reputation to keep. But we must leave so he can do his work."

Outside the ball court, Long Legs noticed a small marketplace. He walked over to view the goods displayed—stone paint palettes and large clam shells with etched designs of lizards and snakes. The centers of some of the shells had been ground out to form bracelets.

Long Legs spoke to one of the local traders. "Where can I trade my rubber balls?" he asked.

I don't know if anyone will trade for them," said the trader. "This might be the last ball game. The town leaders are more interested in building all these platform mounds. This leaves the villagers little time to play their games."

Long Legs walked over to one of the old women displaying her wares. She eyed Squawk who was fiercely gripping Long Legs' shoulder. The boy had, by now, abandoned the birdcage, as Squawk didn't seem to want to leave the travelers even for a moment.

Clutched in the old woman's wrinkled hands was a clay doll in the shape of a ball player. The doll had a tiny shield of clay tied to its left arm and shell anklets on its feet.

"This doll belonged to my grandfather's grandfather," the woman told Long Legs. "They are not made anymore. You'll not find one like this in such good shape. Give me the bird and it's yours."

Long Legs remembered that Little Basket needed a clay doll to offer at the Moonrise—if she survived. He thought carefully, then countered, "I'll give you one old copper bell and two feathers from the macaw."

The old woman agreed, and Squawk lived up to his name while losing his feathers. Long Legs wrapped the doll in a strip of cotton and carefully put it into his pack.

Uncle walked over to Long Legs. "Go and watch the game. I'll trade here for a while," he said. "I'll watch Squawk and your pack."

Feeling helpless about Little Basket, Long Legs squeezed in with the crowd gathered around the ball court. This court had an oval shape instead of being rectangular like the courts at home. He sat next to a boy about his age who had large yellow and red dots painted on his stocky upper body. "My name is Painted Boy," he said, grinning. He explained the game.

"The visiting team will have to give our rulers most of their crops if they lose. But if we lose, we give up nothing. Our city rulers are getting powerful and greedy," Painted Boy continued.

Long Legs said, "Forgive my lack of interest. My sister is in the care of your strange medicine man. I wish I could be with her."

"He'll do his best to heal her—as long as you comply with his wishes," Painted Boy said gravely.

Men and women sitting near Long Legs were making bets on the game. One man, drunk on cactus fruit wine, offered all of his wife's jewelry as a bet, but his friend persuaded him to wager his rabbit-hunting dog instead.

Someone tossed a rubber ball into the court. The players hit it to their teammates, trying to get it to the end of the court that the opposing team was defending. They used their arms, hips, and feet, as no hands were allowed.

A hard-kicked ball hit the head of a player of the visiting team and knocked him out. Friends in the crowd screamed that he was struck on purpose, and several lively fights broke out.

The team of the visiting village lost. Long Legs and Painted Boy watched as they left, carrying their teammate. The losing team was teased by the winning team. "I feel sorry for them," said Painted Boy. "Their families will not have much to eat after they give up their harvest to our village."

Long Legs bade farewell to Painted Boy and rushed back to check on Little Basket. She was awake but looked frightened. Through a weak smile she said, "I'm better."

The medicine man grinned slyly, picking old fur from his coyote skin. "I've decided on a payment," he said. "Your sister says you are going to the Great Salt Bay in search of white clam shells. While there, get me five hundred purple snail shells so I can have new necklaces made." His gnarly fingers fondled a shell string drooping from his neck. After every third shell was a small piece of turquoise. Long Legs recalled that the hostile guard was wearing one just like it.

"We don't have time to find so many shells!" cried Long Legs. "We must be back in eighteen days!" Then, remembering the warning of Painted Boy, he said softly, "But we will be honored to bring them to you."

Chapter 6

Long Legs found Painted Boy at the marketplace bartering for a cape of pelican pelts. The two discussed the medicine man's demand. Painted Boy thought about it. Then he said, "I have been to the Salt Bay many times to gather shells and salt with my father. I'll lead you and your uncle there. Little Basket can stay with my mother. Maybe I can get some pelican pelts from the Salt Bay and not have to trade so much for them."

The three left for the Salt Bay that evening, after settling Little Basket in Painted Boy's house. "Hurry back!" she said faintly as Long Legs squeezed her uninjured hand.

They followed the river southwest through the desert to the Great Bend. Just north of the river were the Travelers' Rocks, smooth boulders capping a lonely hilltop. "Other traders carve animals and designs on the rocks as they pass by. We should carve something for good luck," said Painted Boy.

"No time," said Uncle.

Long Legs was torn. They needed all the luck they could get but dared not waste a minute getting back to

Little Basket. With his finger, Long Legs sketched a design of a desert sheep in the sandy trail. "Please, Sheep Spirit, help Little Basket get better," he whispered.

Leaving the river, which now flowed west, the trio followed a trail south. Giant saguaro cacti lifted huge arms up to a searing blue sky. A family of grunting wild pigs browsed at the trail's edge, eating prickly pear pads, spines and all. Long Legs almost stepped on a fat rattlesnake crossing the trail, but luckily, it slithered peaceably away.

Long Legs sucked a pebble to try to keep the thirst away. He missed the river, and it was a long way between springs. He and Painted Boy insisted that Uncle rest during the worst heat of the day. While Uncle slept in the scant shade of small shrubs, the boys gathered stems of a green-stick bush. They had learned long ago that chewing the raw stems made them salivate more. It was even better than sucking pebbles.

After several days they entered a strange land of black volcanic peaks and gaping craters. Neither water nor the green-stick bush could be seen. As they followed the ancient trail through black crusty soil, Long Legs wondered if they might die of thirst, but his mouth was so dry he could not voice his fears.

"If we don't find water today, we won't make it to the Salt Bay," gasped Uncle as he trudged down the trail.

A flock of birds flew over their heads. "Doves!" cried Painted Boy. "We won't die of thirst after all!"

The boys knew that the doves would be near water. They followed the birds to a deep pool hidden in the sharp cliffs. Carvings of clamshells covered the rock near the pool. "Other shell traders have stopped here," said Painted Boy as they dropped their packs. In seconds, the three were splashing, laughing, and dunking each other.

"Quiet! We have visitors," Uncle said suddenly. Five men with bows and arrows drawn surrounded the pool. Black tattoos covered their glaring faces and gaunt bodies.

While three of them stood guard, the other two dumped the travelers' packs. They grunted in disappointment when they found only a few pouches of corn and mesquite flour.

I'm glad we left all our trade goods at the Big Village, thought Long Legs.

One of the younger tattooed men thrust a knife toward Long Legs, as if he were going to pierce his heart. Long Legs held his breath as he felt the sharp point next to his skin.

An older man, whose entire lower face was tattooed black, spoke sharply to his comrade and grabbed the knife away. Long Legs let out his breath. The older man grunted and motioned to the three in the pool to get out. Then, in sign language, he demanded that the intruders leave the area. The dripping trio hurriedly filled their water pouches, threw on their packs and hastily departed.

By the next afternoon, the black wasteland of the Unfriendly Ones was behind the travelers. Off to the northwest rose a seemingly endless array of giant white sand dunes. Finally, after two more days of jogging, Long Legs smelled salt in the air. Excited, the three ran most of that day and half of the night before they camped.

Long Legs opened his eyes the next morning to a shimmering body of turquoise water that stretched as far as he could see. It was the Great Salt Bay. "There's somebody down by the water!" he said. Grabbing their packs, Painted Boy, Uncle, and Long Legs bounded toward the shoreline, hoping the encounter would be friendlier that the last one.

At the water's edge, a girl struggled with a huge basket full of driftwood. She looked startled as she saw the three travelers loping toward her, but she relaxed as she realized they meant her no harm. She smiled at Long Legs as she hefted the load onto her head ring, her long braids hanging to her waist. Painted purple flowers danced across her pretty brown cheeks when she smiled. In sign language, Long Legs identified his party as traders and asked where they might find white clamshells and purple shells of the sea snail. She motioned to them to follow her.

"I'll find the rest of her people and see if they have pelican pelts," said Painted Boy. He grinned. "I happen to have some chunks of red pigment in my waist pouch that the Unfriendly Ones didn't notice. The chunks will make colorful paint for the braids of the lovely young girls."

Painted Boy darted down the beach while Long Legs and Uncle followed the girl north. As they walked up the shoreline, Long Legs heard giggling from a sandy bluff. He looked up to see two small children sliding down the sandy hill on a sea turtle shell. Just before they reached the edge of the bluff, the pair rolled off, letting the shell drop to the soft sand below.

Long Legs found a clamshell, washed ashore and bleached white by the sun. He looked up. "Look, there are many more farther up the beach!" he cried.

The girl helped fill his pack, padding the shells with long seaweed leaves. She showed the visitors a quiet tide pool where they gathered many purple shells of the sea snail. The girl laughed and pinched her nose, pointing at Long Legs' pack.

"Yes," he nodded to the girl, "they will smell when we get back to the Big Village, but we don't have time to let them dry."

"Where's Painted Boy?" asked Uncle. "We need to start back to Little Basket as soon as possible."

Long Legs squinted as he looked down the sandy beach. A figure with wings was jogging up the shore. As the figure neared, Long Legs saw that it was Painted Boy with a pelican pelt tied to his pack. "They loved the red paint," he laughed. "I saved a small piece for your friend." He handed the girl a tiny chunk of the crumbly rock. She smiled broadly.

Long Legs reached into his waist pouch and drew out the tiny turquoise figure of the bear from the old man of the Mountain People. The girl had saved them much time by showing them where to find the shells, he thought to himself, and he extended his offering to her with a smile. Then, he turned quickly and joined Uncle and Painted Boy for their long journey back.

Nine days later, the exhausted and anxious threesome arrived at the home of Painted Boy. Long Legs burst through the door. Little Basket was grinding corn with Painted Boy's mother. Squawk, perched on her shoulder, shrieked and flew to Long Legs' head where he began to peck happily at his scalp.

"You made it back!" Little Basket cried. "And your pack is full of shells! Let's take them to the medicine man so we can continue our journey. I feel fine. I've even been jogging every day to get back in shape."

Hovering in his room over smelly herbs and animal skins, the old man regarded the pile of shells through slitty eyes. He lit up a reed full of tobacco and said, "These are not enough. You must give me the macaw also. I have never seen such a fine bird. With him, I can be the most powerful medicine man of the Canal People."

Long Legs started to protest but stopped himself, knowing the medicine man would do something awful to them if he didn't obey. He said meekly, "I will bring Squawk to you." The boy left to fetch the bird. He wiped tears of sadness and anger from his eyes as he carried his unsuspecting feathered friend back to the smoky den of the medicine man.

That night, Uncle, Long Legs, and Little Basket said good-bye to the Canal People who had been good to them. "Thank you for leading us to the Great Salt Bay, Painted Boy," said Long Legs. He turned to Painted Boy's mother; "We will never forget how you took such good care of Little Basket."

Then, to avoid any possible confrontations with the medicine man or his guard, they sneaked out of the village. By sunup they were well on their way north.

Little Basket stopped to adjust her forehead strap. A muffled squawk emanated from her pack. "I crept past the mean guard when he was asleep last night. I just had to bring Squawk. I overheard someone say that the medicine man was going to have a huge ceremony and sacrifice the bird. He thinks that will give him great powers from the gods!"

Long Legs felt relief, then worry. "He will surely send someone after us," he said. They all glanced anxiously back down the trail toward the village.

Chapter 7

Leading north from the hot desert, the trail to the Volcano People entered a broad, lush valley. Crimson cliffs towered above corn and cotton fields.

Long Legs was growing concerned about his companions. Uncle stumbled often now and limped as they jogged along the tree-lined path. Little Basket's thin face showed the strain of her recent injury. Sweat poured from under her forehead strap, and Long Legs made her rest often. "We're probably being followed," she'd say after a brief stop. "Let's be on our way."

Squawk, now riding on Long Legs' pack, pecked contentedly at the boy's head, seemingly unaware of potential danger.

They rested once by a pool recessed deep in the earth. Long Legs marveled at the green water gushing from the bottom of the huge well into an irrigation canal. Boys and girls splashed happily in the canal, ignoring the scolds of the irrigators. "I wish the spring that feeds our village canal was as large as this," said Long Legs.

Homesickness and his new responsibilities weighed on him as heavily as the continuous pull of his bulky pack.

One evening, as they climbed the trail out of a red rock canyon, Uncle pointed to the black silhouettes of snow-capped craters in the distance. "The main trading center of the Volcano People lies north of those craters," he said. "That's where we must get the fine cotton cape for an offering at the Moonrise."

The next afternoon, they passed the large dead volcanoes. Pine trees covered the steep slopes, and the air was cool. The trail stretched below into a vast, rainbow-colored desert. A solitary red crater jutted above the desert floor.

All day Long Legs had felt they were being followed. Whenever he'd glance behind him, he could swear he saw the shadow of a figure darting behind a tree or rock at some distance down the trail. He was glad when they reached the trading center north of the red crater at sunset.

The large village seemed to grow out of the red rock ridge that fingered its way through the desert. As they neared the town, Long Legs saw a circular, stonewalled plaza full of traders packing up their goods for the day. Uncle said, "The traders come from the North Country to trade beautiful black-on-white painted pottery for cotton and salt."

Long Legs said, "There are as many traders here as in our village."

"There won't be any spare rooms to sleep in, I'm afraid," said Uncle. "But we shouldn't sleep outside the town, in case we're being followed. Squawk kept looking behind us from your pack all day today. I think he sensed something that we couldn't."

Long Legs didn't comment on what he had seen—or thought he had seen. He didn't want to worry Little Basket more.

That night they slept in a tiny storage room. Uncle and Little Basket fell asleep immediately. Long Legs was crammed between two large jars of dried corn and couldn't stretch out his legs. Mice scurried across the floor and nibbled at spilled beans and corn kernels. When one raced across his face, Long Legs leaped to his feet, moved the flat stone covering the small doorway and stepped outside. Sounds of muffled drums and chanting from a distant ceremonial kiva floated through the sleeping village. He sucked in the cool night air and gazed at the moon. He remembered the woman of the Mountain People telling him about the rabbit in the moon. Sure enough, Long Legs saw it. "Hello, Moon Rabbit," he said. "Two full moons from tonight we need to be at Finger Rocks." As he gazed at the moon, he wondered if they would really make it on time.

Suddenly, he noticed the moonlit shadow of a figure cast against the stonewall. Creeping toward him, the shadow revealed an upraised arm holding a club. Snatching the knife from his waist pouch, Long Legs

whirled around. The dim shape of a tall man disappeared around the corner. The boy tore after him, his heart pounding. As his long stride closed the distance between them, he frantically wondered what he would do if he actually caught up with the man.

As they raced across the plaza, Long Legs leaped for his would-be attacker, grabbing him by the throat. The man jerked away, leaving Long Legs with one of his many necklaces.

Long Legs gasped for air, staring into the dark passageway between the houses where the man had fled. He held the necklaces up to the moonlight. From the broken strings fell purple shells of the ocean snail, plinking lightly on the stone plaza floor. Long Legs stared down. After every third purple shell, a bead of turquoise fell to the ground. Kiva drums beat softly in the distance.

Chapter 8

"It sounds as though he was wearing necklaces like those of the old medicine man," said Little Basket the next morning, as Long Legs told of the frightening encounter. "It must be that horrible guard. He was sent to get Squawk and punish us." She nervously stroked Squawk's head as he perched on her lap. "I shouldn't have risked our lives for him," she said softly. The bird tugged playfully at one of her long braids.

"You can't change the past, Little Basket, but you can influence the future," said Uncle as he rolled up his sleeping mat and tied it to his pack. "If Squawk will kindly donate just a few more feathers, we can trade them for one of the Volcano People's famous cotton capes. It will make a fine offering at the Moonrise Ceremony."

In the plaza Little Basket picked out a beautiful white cape with black zigzag designs. The owner of the cape bartered with Long Legs who translated for Little Basket. "He says you look like his sister. He will take two feathers and three of the salt balls for the cape." Long Legs quickly plucked a scarlet tail feather from an irritated Squawk.

"I spent many nights in the kiva weaving this cape," said the young man as he handed it to Little Basket with a smile. His white teeth flashed in his handsome face. "But I gladly trade it for the salt and the feathers. I belong to the Parrot Clan and tomorrow the entire clan is moving northeast to join our relatives, the Hopi, at Three Mesas."

"What will you do with the feathers?" asked Long Legs, plucking the second from a very vocal Squawk.

"We will use them in the Saqtiva, the Ladder Dance," said the trader.

"May we travel with you to Three Mesas?" asked Long Legs. "They are on the route of our journey. We need to hurry on our way." He looked at Little Basket. "It

would be good to have the company of others, even for a short while..."

"Of course you may travel with us. My name is Weaver."

The trail to Three Mesas crossed a wide yet shallow river and several dry washes that sliced through the shrub-covered desert. Black rain clouds shrouded the high plateau to the northeast, but it was clear and hot where they were hiking. Long Legs, Little Basket, and Uncle were following the last of the Parrot Clan members across a wash when Long Legs noticed a small stream of red-brown water advancing down the arroyo. He heard a low rumble. Suddenly, a frothing brown wall of water came hissing around a corner. A flash flood!

Quickly, Long Legs grabbed the arm of the elderly woman in front of him and pulled her up the steep side of the arroyo. Looking back, he saw Little Basket trying to help Uncle off the ground. He's stumbled again, thought Long Legs as he slid back down the sandy bank. He felt the ground tremble as boulders churned at the head of the floodwater. "Run, Little Basket!" shouted Long Legs. "I'll help Uncle!"

He reached the girl and pushed her toward the bank. She scrambled up, then stared frantically back.

"Go on, Long Legs!" said Uncle. "I've twisted my ankle!" Long Legs flung Uncle's arm over his shoulder and dragged him toward the bank.

"Grab onto that tree root!" said Long Legs. Uncle and Long Legs hoisted themselves up just as the angry water surged by. Large uprooted cottonwood trees thrashed below them in the menacing flood. The little tree jerked and twisted as it bore the weight of the two. Suddenly the tree they were holding onto loosened in the soft soil. Long Legs gritted his teeth and prayed the flood would pass quickly. "It's coming out!" cried Uncle. Then, almost as suddenly as it appeared, the flash flood subsided. The small tree ripped out of the bank and sent the two flying into a shallow stream, red with mud.

Little Basket and the others who were gathered along the rim of the wash burst out in relieved laughter. Uncle and Long Legs dug mud out of their eyes and ears.

Little Basket found a stout cottonwood limb for Uncle to use as a walking stick. "Thank you, my niece," he said. "Though I'm ashamed to have to use this. A good runner shouldn't have to have a cane."

As they continued on the trail, the land seemed barren to Long Legs, but soon the stark shape of one of the Three Mesas came into view. Long Legs wondered why the Parrot Clan wanted to move there instead of the lush valley where the great natural well was. Weaver seemed to sense his curiosity and said, "It seems like bleak country, but the gods have told us to move here. The land of the volcanoes is becoming too crowded, and many people aren't performing our ceremonies correctly." He waved his arm toward Three Mesas. "It won't be so bad. There are springs there and good clay for our pottery."

The tired group of travelers neared Three Mesas. "Most of the villages are at the base of the mesas," said Weaver. "Our clan's village is the only one on the top."

People streamed out of the small stone village perched on the mesa top and filed down the cliff trail. They helped carry packs and dusty children back up to the village.

As the weary Parrot Clan plodded into the plaza to set up a temporary camp, the tired group was greeted by a very old man. Long bangs framed his leathery face, and he wore a black breechcloth and a white cotton blanket. His brown eyes permanently squinted in the dazzling sunlight.

"You are not of our people," he said to Long Legs as the boy clambered up the last of the stone steps. "But welcome!" The old man then turned his kindly face toward Uncle, who was slowly making his way up the trail with his new cane. His pack hung low on his bent back.

"Kokopelli!" the old man cried. He smiled broadly, showing teeth worn down almost to the gums.

Weaver explained to Long Legs, "Kokopelli, one of our spiritual beings, is said to carry a pack full of seeds and often has a cane. He represents fertility and blesses the villages with new babies and a bountiful harvest. Your uncle looks like him."

Purple and black bowls full of corn and rabbit stew were brought to the travelers by young women with large

loops of hair on each side of their heads. "They wind their hair over corn husk frames," said Weaver, noticing Long Legs' curious stare. A girl wearing a black cotton dress attached over the right shoulder, exposing her pretty left arm, shyly handed Long Legs a roll of crisp blue piki bread.

Long Legs smiled at the girl. He looked at the thin, flaky food in his hand. It didn't look like any food he had seen before. "How is this made?" he asked.

The girl stared at the ground as she spoke softly. "The dried blue corn kernels are ground to a powder and mixed with juniper ashes and water. Then, on a flat stone, we spread it out so thinly that you can see through it. A fire burns under the stone, and we turn the thin bread quickly. When it's done, we roll it up like this one." Only when she finished talking did she timidly glance up at Long Legs. Her smile made him blush.

When the girl had left, Weaver said, "Her hair whorls indicate she is not married." He jabbed Long Legs playfully in the ribs.

Resting nearby, Uncle caught Long Legs' eye and smiled at the boy's embarrassment. Long Legs knew Uncle looked forward to the day his nephew would be wed, but he only felt confusion over the prospect. He looked over at Little Basket to see if she had witnessed his conversation with the Hopi girl. She was intently watching a chubby little boy playing near the 500-foot precipice. "Hoya, that small one is so close to the cliff!" said Little Basket, pointing to the child.

Uncle, with Squawk perched on his head, showed no concern. He said, "Children born on the mesa top have no fear of heights." Squawk pecked at the beads woven into Uncle's braid. "I've rarely heard of a child falling off a cliff."

Toward evening, Weaver showed Long Legs and Little Basket where the Ladder Dance was to be held. It would take place over on another mesa. They walked out onto a narrow finger of the ridge. Several men were singing as they erected four spruce trees along the narrow ledge, securing the trunks in round holes chipped deep into the rock. The thin trees had crossbars attached to their tops. Two of the trees had buckskin ropes wound from the cross-bars to the tree bases.

Weaver tried to explain the upcoming event. "Two men each climb a tree. When they get to the top, they bend the trees far out over the cliff. When the tree poles stop swaying, the pole fliers leap from one tree to the other, swapping places in mid-air. While all this is occur-ring, two other pole fliers grab the ends of ropes wound around two other trees. They hang on to the rope ends and fly out beyond the cliff's edge as the ropes unwind, going out in wider circles as they uncoil."

Long Legs was impressed but confused at the descrip-tion of the Ladder Dance. Weaver continued, "We offer the living trees to bring rain to our crops," he said. His hand-some face became serious. "If a flier isn't extremely care-ful, he can be dashed to pieces on the rocks below."

Long Legs asked, "Do you know any of the pole fliers?"

Weaver glanced at him quickly, then gazed out over the cliff. He said, "Messengers came to our old village a moon ago. I have been chosen to be one of the honored fliers." Long Legs looked at him with awe.

Both Little Basket and Uncle needed rest, so the trio of travelers planned to stay a day at Three Mesas. The next morning everyone gathered near the rocky ledge where the Saqtiva was to be held.

The crowd chattered excitedly. Children giggled at Squawk as they tried to get him to repeat their names. Then all grew quiet. Long Legs heard a drum begin to beat, followed by the sound of rattles. Four young men appeared, their bodies painted black. "They are painted as if for death," whispered Uncle.

Long Legs couldn't immediately tell which one was Weaver. All four wore face paint and hawk and eagle feathers woven into their long hair. However, one had an extra feather bound into a long braid on the side—a bright red macaw feather. "May the gods be with you, Weaver," Long Legs said softly.

Two of the fliers climbed to the tops of two spruce trees. They stood upright on the crossbars, facing each other. All Long Legs heard was the creaking of the tree poles as they bent out over the cliff. Finally, the poles stopped swaying. Both young men then leaped from their crossbars. They passed each other in mid-air and grabbed the other's crossbar. The trees bent far over the precipice and then swung back. At the same time, Weaver and the fourth young man ran to the tree poles to which the ropes were tied. Grabbing the rope ends, the two swung out over the valley floor. As the ropes unwound from the poles, Long Legs thought, Weaver flies like an eagle.

The thin trees bent and creaked. Each time Weaver flew out over the edge, Long Legs thought his pole would snap. It seemed like a long time before the ropes unwound completely.

Finally, Weaver and the other flier reached the ground. From behind a rock, four figures with globs of mud for ears, eyes, and mouths appeared.

"The Mudheads!" cried the delighted Hopi children. "Mudheads!" screeched Squawk, perched on Little Basket's shoulder.

The Mudheads playfully grabbed the fliers and dragged them back to the poles. They gestured that they

would show the fliers how to perform the Ladder Dance. Two climbed clumsily up the poles, slipping as they went. The other two grabbed the unwound ropes, tangling themselves completely and nearly falling off the cliff.

Long Legs laughed with the rest of the crowd. Weaver and the other fliers had done well. The crops on Three Mesas would surely have rain this summer.

Chapter 9

"I attended a meeting in the underground kiva last night with the Parrot Clan," said Uncle to Long Legs and Little Basket as they loaded their packs in the plaza. "My nephew, on this trip you have proven to be a brave and thoughtful young man. My legs need to rest. The town elders don't want you and your sister to travel on alone, but, unfortunately, everyone from this village must stay to work in the fields and I must rest. You will have to take Little Basket to the Moonrise yourself."

Little Basket's eyes filled with tears. "We can't leave you here!" she said running to him.

"Little Basket, do not fear for me," said Uncle gently. "The Parrot Clan has offered me their hospitality. I can help quarry stones for the new houses they must build. My hands and arms are still strong, but my legs are not. You and your brother must continue your journey without me."

Uncle escorted his niece and nephew to the trail down the mesa. Pulling Long Legs aside, he said "The men in the kiva described a trader from the South who passed through here last year. Few traders from our area come this far north. This man sounded a lot like your dear father, my sister's husband."

"Where was he headed?" Long Legs asked anxiously.

"He mentioned something about wanting to go east to see the Great Ceremonial Center that is now mostly abandoned. He wondered if anyone remained there who might have fine turquoise to trade."

"We could go there on the way to the Moonrise, couldn't we?" asked Long Legs.

"Of course! You must do everything you can to find your father. It's one of the shortest routes, as well. But hurry on your way. You must travel far each day. Follow the main trail east."

He looked at Little Basket, standing at the mesa's rim and watching them with sad eyes. "Be sure to sleep well off the trail and make Squawk ride backwards to let you know if you are being followed."

"Will we see you again?" sobbed Little Basket as she clung to Uncle at the trailhead.

"When my legs are rested, I will make the long journey home. I hope to see you there by next fall."

Long Legs held Little Basket's hand as they picked their way down the rocky trail off the mesa. When they reached the base of the mesa, he looked back. Uncle's wiry frame shone in the light of the morning sun. He was hunched over his cane, watching them go. "Good-bye, Kokopelli," choked Long Legs. As the trail leveled off, they broke into a trot. Running past small fields of green corn shoots, Long Legs heard the sounds of flute music drifting off the mesa.

Chapter 10

The days faded together as they ran east through pinyon and juniper forests and stark gray deserts. Little Basket padded along, staring at the ground as if in a daze. When they rested, she was disturbingly quiet. Not even Squawk could cheer her up. She moaned often in her sleep but did not share her dreams. Even Long Legs' roasted rabbits did not spark her interest at mealtime.

Long Legs watched the moon every night. It waned, then began to wax, and he knew that they must travel even faster. He tried not to think about what the gods would do to his mother and the other villagers if he did-n't get Little Basket to the ceremony by the time the moon next rose full.

One night, as they ran by the dim light of the half moon, the trail broadened into a wide road. "I could lie across this trail six times," he marveled. "I wonder what purpose it serves."

"Look, Long Legs," said Little Basket. "There's a fire way up on the cliff ahead!" As they passed under the cliff, Long Legs saw another fire burning faintly in the distance.

"The road is marked with fires!" said little Basket.

Or perhaps our arrival is being signaled ahead, thought Long Legs. The two slept little that night. Rising early the next morning, they gazed down the road. It led in a straight line to the base of a cliff where a walled town larger than any Long Legs had ever seen rose from the valley floor. As they approached the huge complex, a strange feeling crept through him. "It's too quiet," he said.

Cautiously, they entered a doorway on the southwest side of the walled town. "We enter in peace!" Long Legs called. "Peace!" screeched Squawk from atop his pack.

They peered down through a series of open doorways connecting empty rooms. "We'll leave our packs here until we find somebody to talk to," said Long Legs. As they walked from room to room, they saw corn-grinding stones lying in kitchen areas. "It looks as if the occupants might come back any minute," Little Basket said nervously.

They climbed through a stone archway. A flat rock slab covered the doorway at the top. Long Legs lifted the heavy rock aside. When they looked through the doorway, they gasped in astonishment. "Look at all those underground ceremonial rooms!" Little Basket whispered.

"Those are called kivas," said Long Legs. "Remember them from the Hopi villages? Wait, what's that noise?" They both listened.

"A drum!" said little Basket. Searching for the rhythmic beat of a muffled drum, they crossed the plaza.

"It's coming from down here," said Long Legs, as he cautiously peered down a ladder hole into a kiva. The drumbeat stopped. After a long silence, a raspy voice called out, "Chiya!"

Long Legs tried to remember the language of the northern people. "I think he said to come down," he told Little Basket.

"I've never been in a kiva," Little Basket said. "Are you sure girls are allowed?"

"Uncle told me girls are allowed for certain ceremonies in some villages. You'll be told if you are not welcome."

They carefully climbed down the ladder into the blackness, choking on the smoke wafting out of the hole. When his eyes adjusted to the dim firelight, Long Legs saw a thin man peering at them from a bench across the kiva. He wore a single-strand necklace, and his breechcloth was tattered and dirty. "My name is Fire Keeper. What brings you children to our vacant town?"

In halting phrases, Long Legs explained their mission. His intuition told him it was safe to tell this man of Little Basket's powers. He concentrated hard on the man's reply.

"I may have heard of your sister. A man from your country was here many moons ago. He was from the Village of Many Houses." Fire Keeper smiled slightly at Long Legs. "He looked a lot like you. He did not mention your sister until the accident."

"What accident?" blurted Long Legs.

"What's he saying?" asked Little Basket.

"Accident!" cried Squawk from his perch on the ladder.

The man continued. "The trader wanted a ceremonial turquoise necklace our people were so famous for. He said he wanted it for his daughter. But there were so few people left, and nobody had any good quality turquoise. The great mine to the southwest closed years ago, about the time our priests lost their power to bring rain to our canyon."

"Accident!" screeched Squawk again through the entrance hole in the kiva roof.

"The trader felt sorry for us. One day he climbed the cliff east of the Great House. He wanted to repair the dam that once captured the rain and diverted it to our fields. He thought if he fixed the dam, the gods might be kind and send rain."

Little Basket nudged Long Legs. He gave her an understanding nod and a look that said, "Be patient."

Fire Keeper continued, "While he was carrying a large rock up the cliff to the old dam, he slipped. He fell a long way. My family took care of him, but he never was quite right after that." Fire Keeper looked at Little Basket. "He kept telling us his daughter had great powers and the gods responded to her offerings. He said she could help us."

"He could be our father," said Long Legs. "Where is he now?"

"One day he disappeared. Soon after that, almost everyone in the entire canyon and beyond moved away, even my family. Just a few of us remained. I stayed to guard the kivas and the Great House. The fireguards light fires on the cliffs above the roads to warn me of approaching strangers."

"Do you have many visitors?"

"Hardly any, until yesterday. A strange and sinister man came looking for three travelers. He frightened me, but I admired his necklaces. He agreed to trade one of them." He held up a familiar-looking string of beads.

Long Legs walked over to the man and studied the necklace. It was made of purple shells and after every third bead was a bead of turquoise. "I haven't seen turquoise in a long time," Fire Keeper sighed.

"Where did this man go?" asked Long Legs nervously.

"I don't know which direction he went. When I told him I had seen no one in many moons, he said he'd find them anyway."

"We must leave now," said Long Legs. "If Little Basket is not at Finger Rocks when the full moon rises between them, more people than just Little Basket and I will suffer."

"From what your father said, your sister may be able to help my people still living in the Far North. I'll travel with you to Finger Rocks."

Fire Keeper packed some dried rabbit meat in a tattered cloth and was ready. Long Legs and Little Basket retrieved their packs and the trio headed north on the wide, straight road.

"I had almost forgotten about the man who was following us," said Little Basket when Long Legs told her about the kiva conversation. "Oh, Long Legs, do you think

Father might still be alive somewhere? He won't know how to find his way home!"

Scrubby pinyon and juniper trees lined the road. The three travelers slept only in the heat of the afternoon, in sheltered areas away from the trail. After three days, Long Legs noticed the fields again. Young boys scurried from the field houses. They yelled at crows and ravens that were pecking on young cobs of colorful corn.

"The large village that replaced ours as the new center of power is up ahead along the river," said Fire Keeper.

When they entered the plaza, Long Legs was amazed at the variety of people. "Many have traveled far to attend the Moonrise," said Fire Keeper. "This is the last major town on their route. They might have a ceremony in the Great Kiva here tonight to celebrate the forthcoming Moonrise at Finger Rocks. I'm sure you and Little Basket could attend."

That night Long Legs marveled at the size of the Great Kiva as he listened to the pounding of the huge foot drums. Fire Keeper lamented, "We have a kiva larger than this across the canyon from the Great House where you found me. Many of the older priests you see here tonight used to sing there. Only the wind sings there now." He stared sadly at the floor.

Long Legs noticed that Little Basket was gazing, transfixed, into the fire. She murmured strange words in a low, eerie voice. Her eyes closed, and she slumped against him. The gods are already talking to her, he thought. I wish we could go straight to Finger Rocks instead of the place of the Cliff Dwellers. It is so out of the way. Little Basket is getting so weak.

He picked her up and carried her outside. Finding the camp where visitors stayed, he placed her on her sleeping mat. She chanted the strange words in her sleep. Long Legs looked at the moon. In nine days the moon will be full, he thought. "I hope Little Basket doesn't get worse," he said softly to Squawk.

Chapter 11

His rabbit fur blanket crunched with a frost crust when Long Legs awoke. The eastern sky was already crimson. "Wake up, Little Basket! We have to get to the mesas of the Cliff Dwellers in less than five days!" If she were in good health that would be no problem, he thought.

Fire Keeper came over, looking concerned when he saw the weary Little Basket. "Take care of her, Long Legs. I'm sorry I can't go with you, but I'm heading northeast with the others toward Finger Rocks. I'm too old to make the detour you have to make. Just follow the main trail west, then head north when Rock Mountain becomes visible to the southwest."

Long Legs had hoped that Fire Keeper would accompany them in case the guard from the Canal People's medicine man was still pursuing them. He sighed and helped Little Basket arrange her pack. He put the moon rabbit bowl and the clay ball player in his own pack and said as merrily as possible, "Good thing we only have one more place to trade. We don't need any more weight." But Little Basket only looked at him with vacant eyes.

Long Legs resented every step as it led them in the opposite direction of their destination. Several times he stopped, resolved to turn around and go to Finger Rocks without the mug they needed from the Cliff Dwellers. Each time, however, he visualized Thunder Voice peering at Little Basket's offerings, rage in his face upon discovering the mug's absence. Fear of what he'd do to Little Basket kept Long Legs moving forward again toward the mesas of the Cliff Dwellers.

As the autumn sun rose over the golden desert, it reflected hot off a sandstone cliff that paralleled the travelers' route much of the morning. Picture carvings covered the rock, most very worn but a few freshly pecked. An isolated boulder lay close to the trail. "Let's rest under the shade of this boulder, Little Basket. We can look at the old picture carvings."

Little Basket slumped in the shade while Long Legs inspected the carvings. He heard a rustling movement on the other side of the rock. A rattlesnake slithered from behind the rock toward Little Basket.

"Don't move, Little Basket," Long Legs whispered. "The snake won't bother us if we don't frighten it."

Something has already frightened it, he thought. He cautiously crept along the boulder, careful not to disturb the snake. He peeked around the corner.

Suddenly, a shape moved from behind the boulder. A shirtless man with tattoos covering his face, arms, and chest stepped in front of them.

He held a drawn bow, the arrow aimed at Little Basket. Squawk, sitting on Little Basket's pack, screeched nervously.

"I've finally found you children alone!" he rasped. "That stupid bird makes it impossible to sneak up behind you. Nobody gets away with humiliating the great medicine man of the Canal People. He will be pleased to get the red bird back to sacrifice. Its death will give him even more powers."

The guard glanced at Little Basket slumped weakly against the boulder. "He will also enjoy knowing that the ungrateful child who stole part of his payment for making her well is not so well anymore. In fact, it will give me great pleasure to tell him that both of your bodies are nothing more than raven food."

"Don't do it," said Long Legs quietly. "If you make a sudden move, that rattlesnake next to your foot will strike."

The tattooed man's thin lips curled up in a wicked grin. "The boy who thinks he's a man tries to fool me! This will make the killing even more pleasurable."

A rattling noise at his feet distracted him. The snake was coiled, ready to strike. Its flat, triangular head weaved slightly back and forth, as if taking aim at the man's muscular calf. A forked tongue flicked in and out.

"Get a rock and kill it!" the man cried, frozen with the bow in his hands.

Long Legs hesitated. They would be killed if he saved him. The guard obviously knew what was going through Long Legs' head. He suddenly whirled sideways and shot the arrow at the snake. As the arrow harmlessly stuck in the sand, the rattler struck. The guard grabbed his leg, screaming in pain and horror.

"Run, Little Basket!" Long Legs grabbed her hand and pulled her away, going around the man and the snake at a safe distance. He then raced back for the packs and Squawk.

The guard reached out a tattooed hand and grabbed Long Legs' ankle as he retreated. Long Legs wrenched free and kicked sand at the guard. The man clawed at his eyes, as he writhed on the ground and screamed curses at Long Legs.

When they could no longer hear his cries, Long Legs stopped running and made Little Basket rest. She talked little, and Long Legs could not read her face. It seemed absent of emotion. Was the poison of the giant lizard still in her blood? Was it fatigue from the trip, or fear of the tattooed man? Were the gods talking to her? Whatever it was, Long Legs knew they had to move quickly, get the mug from the Cliff Dwellers, and get to the Moonrise Ceremony, without killing Little Basket doing it. After a few minutes, the two resumed a slow jog forward.

Looming in the hazy distance to the southwest was a huge, isolated rock. "That must be Rock Mountain, Little Basket! We'll camp as soon as the sun goes down and be at the mesas of the Cliff Dwellers in two days."

Little Basket did not appear to hear him. Long Legs got behind her and winced as he saw her shuffling along as fast as she could, her skinny legs looking stick-like below the big pack. He stopped and tied her sleeping mat and the cotton cape of the Volcano People to the top of his pack. There was little left in her pack but extra sandals, some dried meat, sunflower seeds, pinyon nuts, a bladder bag of water, and her rabbit fur blanket. Long Legs tied the water bag to his pack and made a disheveled Squawk ride on his pack. He wanted to make his sister's pack as light as possible.

Across the high desert Long Legs could see smoke filling the broad valley to the northwest. There must be more people living there than I've seen in a lifetime, he thought. He longed to head straight for the towns ahead but knew they had to climb the mesa to the north.

Toward nightfall of the next day they couldn't find even a stunted juniper to sleep under. "Look at all the stumps, Little Basket. There's hardly a living tree to be seen." As Little Basket slept fitfully on her rabbit fur blanket, Long Legs stared up at the huge flat mesa to the north, trying to imagine what the people were like who were moving into the cliff caves. He tried to think of anything but sleep. He knew the guard was probably disabled or dead, but he was still nervous.

"Help me listen for unusual noises," he told Squawk as the bird snuggled next to the girl's head. Long Legs promptly fell asleep.

The next morning was colder than the one before. Long Legs felt sorry for Little Basket as she shivered in the dim light while trying to put her rabbit fur blanket around her slim shoulders and under the cumbersome pack. Although she had slept most of the night, she did not respond to her brother's attempt at conversation.

They followed the main trail north to a small river. Its broad bed told of a time when the river had run much wider. The path followed the river northeast. As they came closer to it, the mesa didn't look like a single land mass any more. Instead, a series of long skinny fingers snaked south toward them. In mid-afternoon Long Legs spotted a trail veering toward one of the mesas. "I don't know where the Cliff Dwellers live. We'll just hope this trail leads us to some of them. It will be a steep climb, Little Basket," Long Legs said worriedly.

"Steep climb!" shrieked Squawk as they left the well-worn path along the river. Little Basket stumbled frequently and had to rest often as they climbed the rocky trail. Long Legs noticed that even many of the scrubby little trees on the steep talus slope had been cut.

The sun was setting when they finally reached the mesa top. After giving Little Basket some water, Long Legs allowed himself a look around. In wonder, he saw that the entire mesa was covered with fields of corn, beans, and squash. People were stooped over in the fields, gathering the harvest in huge baskets hung on their backs with forehead straps. Scattered among the fields were small clusters of rock houses one to three stories high, some in ruins, others with people, dogs, and turkeys milling about. Hardly a juniper or pinyon tree was in sight.

A polite cough behind him startled Long Legs. A young man with a digging stick stood a short ways from him and Little Basket. Although he looked sympathetically at the exhausted girl, he held the stick as if to defend himself. In sign language he asked Long Legs where they were from and what they were doing there. Long Legs attempted to answer in the language of the people of the Far North.

"We have come from a village a long way to the south. We need to trade for a fine mug of a Cliff Dweller in order to offer it at the Moonrise Ceremony at Finger Rocks. My sister is sick and needs food and rest. Will you help us?"

The young man seemed intrigued with Long Legs' accent. "You speak our language well for a foreigner. Follow this path north along the rim. I'll tell you when to stop." Long Legs helped his sister to her feet and steadied her along the trail until he was sure she was stable. The man followed behind them.

Where the mesa began its slope towards the rim, Long Legs noticed that every little gully had several small dams of piled rocks spanning it. Upslope from each little dam, several corn plants were growing in the soil that had washed down. The man behind Long Legs noted his interest and said, "Each year we lose more soil as the rains wash it away. Some say it's because we've cut all the trees and there's nothing to hold it anymore. We try to keep the soil on the mesa with these little dams and plant some of our crops behind them." Long Legs thought the corn plants looked spindly and unhealthy compared to the corn he picked at home during harvest time.

Up ahead Long Legs saw a group of rock buildings. The young farmer behind him said, "The village leaders assemble here. We'll tell them you're here."

All Long Legs wanted to do was to get Little Basket fed and rested, but he was in no position to argue. He gently told Little Basket to turn toward the buildings. A black and white longhaired dog trotted happily over to Little Basket, but she stared straight ahead as if she saw nothing.

"Turn into this room." The two stooped through the T-shaped doorway. Long Legs adjusted his eyes to the dim light and choked involuntarily on the smoke. He saw several men clustered near a fire hearth in the corner of the room, squatting in the same position all people did in low-ceilinged rooms. Their voices seemed strained. He caught a few words and guessed they were arguing about water.

The young man with the digging stick said, "Many of our springs are drying up where we get our drinking water. Some people are moving down into the cliff overhangs where the springs are, to protect them from other villagers. The village leaders disagree on who should live closest to the springs and control the water. Also, our crops aren't doing well, and the people don't want to share their food like they used to." The young man looked worried. "Bands of hungry strangers have been stealing from the villages in the valley below. It's thought we can better protect our stored food in the cliffs, away from the strangers and perhaps from each other."

The men looked startled as they glanced up at Long Legs and Little Basket. An older man with wild gray hair motioned at them with a withered arm to take off their packs and squat down with them. He smiled kindly at Little Basket. Long Legs noticed that most of his teeth were worn down to the gums. Squawk flew off of Long Legs' shoulder and landed on the old man's head. He laughed and tried to pet the bird, who immediately nipped at his fingers.

Long Legs explained the reason for their visit. "I know where you may find the perfect mug for the offering," the elder said. "Your sister can rest here while I take you there. We will feed her. Then she'll sleep easily with the drone of all these serious men talking about local matters."

Long Legs settled Little Basket in a corner on her blanket with a bowl of corn mush. The longhaired dog had followed her in and curled up next to her. Little Basket looked at it blankly, yet flung her arm over it when she lay down.

Long Legs followed the man outside and toward the cliff, noticing that one of the elder's legs was shorter than the other. As if he'd sensed his question, the man said, "I don't like the idea of moving off the mesa from our cozy houses and into these miserable overhangs in the cliffs. I broke my leg falling off this hand-and-toe-hole trail several years ago. These places aren't fit for anyone but the young and foolish. Here's the trail. Be careful climbing down. I'll go first." The man disappeared over the cliff.

Long Legs warily dangled a leg over the cliff and felt for the small step that had been carved into the rock. His other foot groped for the indented step below. The partial

moon was just coming up but didn't light the cliff face below him. "This would be bad enough in daylight, but I really can't see what's below me in the dark," he mumbled as he slowly made his way dawn the cliff face. "How do little children get down here? Or people carrying firewood or deer meat or ..." Thud! Missing a step, Long Legs crashed to the ground at the feet of the old man.

"No broken bones? Then come this way." Long Legs brushed himself off and limped after the elder toward the side of the huge recess in the cliff. The moonlight was blocked off from the cliff, making it darker. The sun probably doesn't shine here until late afternoon, he thought grimly.

A sudden breeze brought the stench of garbage and human waste to his nose. The old man said, "Another reason I hate these cliff dwellings is that the only place you can throw your garbage is in front of your house."

The sound of chanting rose from a kiva smoke hole. The man skirted around the kiva and headed across a courtyard for the far end of the overhang. Long Legs heard the talking and laughing of families as he passed by the little rooms snuggled against the back of the overhang. The evening wind whipped sharply through the overhang. He felt terribly cold and very homesick.

"Here we are. Good, she's home. Mug Woman, may we enter?" A woman's voice replied, and the elder pulled back the cloth door. A large slab rested next to the outside of the doorway. Just like our winter doors, Long Legs thought. He followed the elder into the smoky room. The squeal of children greeted him, and, through the veil of smoke, he saw several little bodies squirm through the T-shaped doorway into the next room.

He squatted on the hard mud floor and looked at the woman across from him. Her face was weathered but pleasant. She wore her hair short, with bangs. Long Legs remembered the shy, unmarried Hopi girl with the huge hair whorls. Weaver had told him that after girls married they often cut their hair off and used it to make twine and nets to catch rabbits.

The old man explained to the woman that Long Legs needed a mug for his sister to offer at the Moonrise Ceremony. The woman called to the children in the next room.

A pudgy child of about five years peeked shyly through the small doorway and immediately withdrew. "The stranger won't hurt you. Look! He has a big red bird on his shoulder! Bring some of my new mugs for him to look at."

A rustling was heard. Then a little girl appeared with a mug in each hand. She carefully climbed over the bottom of the T-shaped doorway and walked slowly toward Long Legs, watching the mugs intently as if that would keep them from dropping. Next came a younger boy who held a mug carefully in both hands, his little face screwed up in concentration as he carried it to Long Legs. The next child was older and carried five mugs tied together with yucca twine. They retreated to the other room and the same process was repeated. Soon there were more than sixteen mugs awaiting Long Legs' inspection, all white and painted in black with elaborate designs of triangles, small squares, zigzags, and scrolls.

The old man chuckled and said, "The women in this cliff dwelling are known throughout the mesas for making the finest mugs. Mug Woman and her cousin paint the best designs. The gods will appreciate an offering of any one of these."

Long Legs picked one up. The flat base was larger than his palm and the sides were tapered to a flat rim. The handle started at the rim and curved down all the way to the base. Long Legs thought of the rounded ladles his family used for dipping water from jars. The mugs could be set flat on the ground. I'll have to tell mother about these, he thought. Another wave of homesickness washed over him.

The smallest child crawled into Long Legs' lap, reaching up to his shoulder to pet Squawk. The macaw nibbled gently at his fat fingers. Laughing, the little one withdrew his hand and reached for a nearby mug. As he picked it up, the one beside it rose as well. They were connected to each other where their handles would have been. "That's the one we'll take," declared Long Legs. The child's big brown eyes lit up in glee under his long bangs. He carefully handed the double mug to Long Legs, giggled, and tottered over to his mother.

"What do you have to trade for it?" the woman asked Long Legs as she cuddled the little boy in her arms. Long Legs looked at her plain necklace of white snail shells and wished he could offer some of the turquoise jewelry he'd already traded away.

"All I have left to trade is a feather from Squawk." He thought he felt the bird stiffen at the mention of his name. The woman's eyes widened.

"We could tie it to the prayer stick in our sleeping room. The little ones would have nice dreams." Long Legs was glad she didn't want more than one feather. Squawk was looking less fluffy every day.

When Long Legs and a thinner Squawk returned to Little Basket, it was after midnight. Although he felt fairly safe, Long Legs barely slept. Several village representatives were sleeping in the next room and snored so loudly that Squawk started imitating them. Long Legs wanted to move outside but didn't want to wake Little Basket. Squawk shortly became bored and quieted down, but the din in the next room kept Long Legs awake the rest of the night.

Little Basket showed a spark of pleasure when she saw the double mug as they packed to leave the next morning. But as they wound down the trail along the sandstone rim, she became silent and distant again.

The old man who had taken Long Legs to the Cliff Dwelling led them through a stunted cornfield to a trail on the other side of the mesa. "This is a shorter trail back to the river you were following yesterday. Keep following it upstream to its headwaters. The trail heads east over several small mountain ranges and ends up at Finger Rocks. I hope Little Basket's offerings please the gods. If they don't, we all might have to move into those wretched cliff dwellings!"

They hiked off the mesa and then followed the shallow river to the top of a narrow range of mountains. There were a few small communities along the way, but they dared not stop. They had only four more days to get to the Moonrise Ceremony. Long Legs noticed that most of the little towns had been abandoned, some probably before he was born. He wondered why the Far North People seemed to be gathering together in larger communities. Were they afraid of the strangers or each other? He was stunned by the number of trees that had been cut, even at great distances from the villages.

They encountered other people heading toward Finger Rocks. Long Legs was tempted to ask them for help, but he wasn't sure what they could do. Little Basket had to present the offerings herself.

On the fourth night they camped on the east side of another low mountain range. Little Basket had not spoken to Long Legs for two days but kept mumbling to herself. She chanted strange words again in her sleep. She is talking with the gods all the time now, thought Long Legs. He slept little and the next morning woke up so exhausted that he feared neither one of them would make it to Finger Rocks.

He reached over and tugged at his sister's skinny arm sticking out from under her rabbit fur blanket. "Time to get up, Little Basket. We should get to Finger Rocks tonight if we hurry!" Her eyes slowly opened. Long Legs gasped. They were so bloodshot that they looked pure red. They stared wildly at him as if she didn't know who he was. When she tried to get up, she yelled something he couldn't understand and slumped to the ground, unconscious.

Long Legs tried to calm the panic growing inside him. He covered up his sister with her blanket and frantically looked around for some fallen aspen trees that may have been missed for firewood. He finally found two long poles. Laying them side-by-side, he tied them apart at one end a little wider than his waist and at the opposite end a bit farther apart. Quickly, he wove some branches between the poles. He placed Little Basket and her pack on the crude carrier. He picked up the narrower end, a pole in each hand, and began to drag the carrier down the trail.

Squawk flew up to his head, but Long Legs brushed the bird off. "Sorry, old friend, I don't want your claws digging into my head today." Squawk snorted and flew back to the carrier, where he perched on Little Basket's stomach. Long Legs glanced back at them. Squawk's red feathers were certainly more ruffled and scruffy than they had been at the beginning of the journey. Even Squawk is exhausted, he thought.

At midday Long Legs saw a lone pinyon pine tree a short distance off the trail. He dragged the carrier over to it. He could walk no further. Making sure Little Basket's face was in the shade, he lay down next to the carrier. Squawk nestled next to him but looked up suddenly. Long Legs thought he saw something flash behind the tree. He tried to focus but his vision grew blurry. "Little Basket..." he muttered, but his voice faded into the depths of sleep.

Chapter 12

Long Legs opened his eyes. The sun had traveled far across the sky during his nap. He bounded up and stared at the pole carrier. Little Basket, his pack, and Squawk were gone! He frantically searched for clues and noticed large sandal tracks by the carrier. He studied the tracks carefully. Whoever took Little Basket is wearing sandals so worn that his toes touch the ground, he thought. Hoya, I wish I hadn't fallen asleep!

Long Legs raced east, following the tracks in the sandy road. He's taking her to Finger Rocks, Long Legs thought.

The sun was only a fist above the horizon when he finally saw the tall spires of the two Finger Rocks. They towered majestically atop a ridge, high above the valley floor. Long Legs saw the small shapes of many people gathered near the spires.

Suddenly, from behind a twisted juniper tree, a man leaped out and grabbed Long Legs by the throat, dragged him to the ground and began choking him. Long Legs struggled for his knife, but the man had pinned his arms with his massive legs. Long Legs thought his ribs would snap.

The man with the tattoo-covered face sneered and jabbed his legs harder into Long Legs' ribs. "You thought you'd left me for dead, didn't you? I guess that snake had used its poison on some poor rabbit and had little left for me." Long Legs felt himself losing consciousness as the man's fingers dug into his throat. Everything was blurred except the necklace of purple shells and turquoise beads hanging from the thick neck above him.

Abruptly, the death grip loosened. The man slumped to his side and Long Legs gasped for air. His attacker lay next to him, a huge rock beside his bloody head. Long Legs could see no movement in the man's chest. The evil guard was dead.

Long Legs staggered to his feet. A thin man was running down the trail. "Wait!" Long Legs called, but the man didn't stop. He wore a ragged kilt and his long hair was matted and wild.

Long Legs followed his rescuer up the winding trail to the ridge top. A stone village of empty rooms was spread along the narrow ridge. The man disappeared into the crowd gathered near Finger Rocks. Long Legs scanned the faces in the crowd. The man might have seen Little Basket, he thought.

A fearsome voice boomed from the base of the Finger Rocks. "Our sun leaves Father Sky to make way for Moon.

Every nineteen years offerings are placed at the altar to make Moon rise between the Finger Rocks."

Long Legs observed the owner of the voice. Necklaces of knucklebones covered his massive chest and he wore an elaborate feathered headdress. His thick black hair almost touched the ground. He was taller than anyone Long Legs had seen. The silent crowd stared in wonder and fear at him. "Thunder Voice," guessed Long Legs.

The priest continued. "The medicine girl from the South Country did not arrive with the offerings we requested. We hope the Moon will still rise and linger between the spires. If not, we fear all the North Country will soon be abandoned, such as what happened here at the old village of Finger Rocks."

Long Legs' heart pounded so loudly he was certain those around him could hear it. He listened carefully as Thunder Voice finished his speech.

"Our brothers of the Great Ceremonial Center displeased the gods. Their farmland is spoiled, their village deserted." He waved his arms at the vacant houses. "Even this village, which was built to supply the Great Ceremonial Center with wood beams, lies in ruins. Our brothers to the west fight among themselves for food. Some want to move into the cliff overhangs to protect themselves from their neighbors."

Long Legs felt a tap on his shoulder. He turned to see a familiar face. "I am Raven Claw. I was at your village many moons ago requesting the presence of your sister here," he said. "Where is she? The priests are angry she did not come. I fear you and your family will suffer."

"She almost made it but someone took her," Long Legs stammered. "I don't know..."

There was a commotion near the altar. A man with half his body and face painted black approached Thunder Voice and whispered something to him. The priest looked startled. The painted man darted back into the crowd. Shortly, he and another man emerged, supporting the body of a girl. Long Legs squinted. A red bird perched on the girl's limp shoulder.

"Little Basket!" Long Legs cried. He tried to push his way through the crowd toward the altar, but the spectators were jammed so tightly together he couldn't move. He yelled again for his sister. Drums started to pound, and the priests began to chant, drowning out his cries.

The painted man and another with ragged clothes and unkempt hair carried Little Basket to the altar. Long Legs felt a flood of relief as he saw her try to stand by herself. The skinny man with the wild hair stood next to her, holding her whenever she wavered. His long matted hair covered most of his face. That is the man who rescued me, thought Long Legs.

Someone presented Little Basket with Long Legs' pack, and the ragged man helped her open it. One by one, she gently placed on the altar the bowl with the painted moon rabbit from the Mountain People, the ancient clay doll from the Canal People, the white cotton cape from the Volcano People, the white clamshells from the Great Salt Bay, and the double mug from the Cliff Dwellers. She stumbled back from the altar. The crowd joined the priests in their chant. The moon edged between the two spires. The drums beat louder. Little Basket raised her thin arms toward the moon. It exploded white and huge between the rocks.

Silence settled over the crowd. In a voice strange and distant, Little Basket spoke. "I have visited with the gods during the last few days. They gave me a message to give to you." She paused to gather strength. The thin man beside her translated her words to Thunder Voice.

Little Basket continued slowly. "The gods are not punishing you. They are telling you that you have been in one place too long." The moon traveled higher between the rocks, then appeared to stand still. The crowd gasped and then stared back at Little Basket. She continued. "Your numbers are too great, and you are out of balance with the plants and animals." Thunder Voice studied the girl intently as her words were translated. "Soon you will tire of quarreling among yourselves for food, and the gods will give you a sign that it is time to move. The Hopi Parrot Clan has fulfilled its migration promises. You will have to do the same."

Thunder Voice asked sternly, "Where will we go?"

"You will know when the time comes. You will survive. The gods have willed it."

The crowd was silent. The full moon began to move again, squeezing upward between the rock spires.

"It will be so, if the gods so desire," said Thunder Voice. "We will not argue with the gods when they tell us to leave. Let us thank them and the moon. We will feast in their honor."

The people burst into a high-pitched "Eee-iii" and began to disperse. Long Legs pushed through the crowd toward the altar.

"Little Basket!" he shouted. "Are you alright?" She turned her face toward him, her eyes searching his eager face. Finally, she flashed a smile of recognition and hugged him tightly.

"I'm so glad to see you!" she said. Squawk flew from her shoulder and landed noisily on the boy's head. Long Legs noticed the ragged man making his way through the crowd.

"Come back!" he cried. "Stay here, Little Basket. I have to thank that man for saving my life." He sped after him. Little Basket hesitated, then followed.

It was easy to follow the man by moonlight. The ridge narrowed as the trail led them down. Suddenly, off to the right, Long Legs saw a figure crouched behind the branches of a tree. "Please come out, we want to talk to you," said Long Legs.

The thin man moved out into the open. Little Basket walked down the trail toward him. The man turned his head away. Slowly, Little Basket stepped close and gently pulled the tangled hair from his face. Long Legs heard her gasp.

"Father!" she cried. The man stood frozen. Long Legs rushed down the trail.

"Father, don't you know us? We're your children!" he said. The man turned his face toward them. Fear and confusion showed in his eyes. A tear rolled down his dirty cheek.

"Yes, I know you," he finally said. "I am ashamed to have you see me this way."

"We heard what happened to you. We are so proud of you," said Long Legs.

Little Basket reached up and wiped the tear from his cheek. "We'll take you home and make you well again. We need you!"

Long Legs said, "You were the one who brought Little Basket to the ceremony, weren't you?"

"Yes," said his father. "I heard rumors that a young medicine girl from the South Country was coming. I blame myself for the difficult journey. I must have told of your powers, Little Basket, while recovering from my fall. I cannot remember things well."

Little Basket put her arm around his thin waist. Squawk leaped from her shoulder onto his matted head.

Their father smiled. Then his expression turned serious as he said, "I came to Finger Rocks to see if it was really my daughter who was coming. When you didn't arrive, I looked for you. I found you both sleeping near the trail. I could carry only one of you at a time, so I brought Little Basket and the pack with the offerings. The priests were angry that you weren't here yet."

Long Legs said, "Then you returned for me and saved me from the man of the Canal People. He was after Little Basket for stealing Squawk from a medicine man when she heard he would be sacrificed."

"Squawk good bird!" said Squawk, as he fluttered over to Little Basket's shoulder.

"I have never killed a man," said Father. "But this man was going to kill you, my son." He looked at Long Legs fondly. "Why didn't my wife's brother guide you here?"

"He came as far as the Hopi villages, but his legs gave out. He will journey home when he feels stronger." Long Legs put his arm around his father's thin shoulders. "Let's camp below the ridge of the Finger Rocks," he said. "The people will sing all night up here and it would be difficult to sleep. We need rest for our long trip home."

Long Legs and Little Basket gently turned their father around. Little Basket took his hand and led him down the trail. Long Legs followed.

At a bend in the trail, Long Legs stopped and looked back toward Finger Rocks. The full moon rose above them. He smiled as he found the grey shape of the moon rabbit. "Thank you, my friend. Our journey was a success." Long Legs turned and followed his father, sister, and Squawk down the moonlit trail.

Places Visited by Long Legs and Little Basket

Casas Grandes, Chihuahua, Mexico, 100 mi. S of the NM border (where the children lived): Visit the largest trading center in northern Mexico, which linked the cultures of Mesoamerica with the Pueblo towns to the north. Motel nearby.

Gila Cliff Dwellings National Monument, NE of Silver City, NM (north of where the Mountain People lived): Follow the Mimbres River, where the Mimbreno people farmed and painted their fanciful bowls. The cliff dwellings were occupied later by Ancestral Puebloans from the north.

Pueblo Grande Museum, Phoenix, AZ (where the mean Medicine Man lived): Visit the pueblo, ball court, and irrigation canals used by the Hohokam (Canal People).

Wupatki National Monument, N of Flagstaff, AZ (where Weaver lived): See the trading center and numerous ruins of the Sinagua (Volcano People). Sunset Crater looms to the south.

Hopi Villages, E of Flagstaff, AZ (where the Ladder Dance was held): Ask at the Second Mesa Motel how you may visit the oldest continuously occupied villages in the United States.

Chaco Canyon National Historical Park, NM (where Fire Keeper lived): Visit the four-story Pueblo Bonito, which may have been a redistribution center for food, wood, and turquoise for hundreds of smaller villages.

Mesa Verde National Park, near Cortez, CO (where the double-mug was purchased): Tour cliff dwellings below the mesas where the Ancestral Puebloans farmed for more than one thousand years.

Chimney Rock, near Pagosa Springs, CO (Finger Rocks, where the Moonrise occurred): Tour the ruin of the ancient ceremonial site from which can be viewed the rising of the full moon between two spires every 18 years.

Teacher's/Parent's Guide Available!

Summaries of the major cultural groups (the Mogollon, Hohokam, Sinagua, and Ancestral Puebloan) visited by our heroes, Long Legs and Little Basket, are presented in this guide, providing important background information. The guide is set up with the intention of having the teacher, parents, or students read a chapter each day. Discussion questions, research topics, individual activities, group activities, references, and places to visit are provided for each chapter. Projects target 4th through 8th grade students and range from being very simple to requiring more preparation and imagination.

The Guide is available free-of-charge in hard-copy form or for $7.00 on a CD. To order, call Western Reflections Publishing at 1-800-993-4490.

Sally Crum
Author

Western Colorado and the Four Corners area of the Southwest have been home to Sally for more than twenty-five years. She has been an interpretive ranger for the Park Service at several parks, including Mesa Verde, but most of her work has involved archaeological surveys for private contractors, the Navajo Nation, and the U.S. Forest Service. Through her writing, Sally strives to make history and archaeology exciting for the public, especially children. She also has published *People of the Red Earth, American Indians of Colorado*.

Eric Carlson
Illustrator

Eric was born and raised in Juneau, Alaska, and was strongly influenced by the rich native cultures and environment of the Northwest Coast. His educational background in psychology and anthropology further prepared him for employment as an archaeologist and illustrator of artifacts, which he pursues across the West and as far away as the Dead Sea Basin in Jordan. His illustrations have been published in and on the covers of many scientific texts. Eric currently resides in Colorado.

If you enjoyed *Race to the Moonrise,* you may like reading these other children's titles in our "Children of Colorado Series" from Western Reflections Publishing Co.:

Denver Days — In 1882, ten-year-old Katie moves to Denver to work for a well-loved black woman named Aunt Clara Brown. There she tastes her first ice cream soda, meets her first Native American, and learns to ride a bicycle.

A Cabin in Cripple Creek — An adventure story set in 1895, the tale begins when Mary Haskins and her family move to Cripple Creek, Colorado, where she witnesses two big fires that threaten to burn down the entire town.

One Golden Summer — A Ute Indian chief, a Pinkerton detective, a wild pig, and a cantankerous burro all help to keep mischievous Daniel Blair from getting bored in Golden, Colorado, during the summer of 1873.

Daisy the Cripple Creek Donkey — While visiting his grandfather in the mountains of Colorado, Adam develops a close relationship with a donkey who lives in the wild and whose ancestors had worked to pack ore out of the nearby mines.